LONG AGO, SHORTLY AFTER THE BIRTH OF THE UNITED STATES OF AMERICA, WHEN GEORGE WASHINGTON WAS STILL SERVING AS THE FIRST PRESIDENT, THAT IS WHEN THE STORY I AM TELLING YOU, DEAR READER, WAS FIRST TOLD.

IN A QUIET VALLEY, NOT FAR NORTH FROM THE GREAT CITY OF NEW YORK, LIES THE VILLAGE OF *SLEEPY HOLLOW*. IT IS A PLACE KNOWN FOR ITS *PEACE* AND THE UNUSUAL *CHARACTERS* WHO LIVE THERE.

A DROWSY, DREAMY INFLUENCE SEEMS TO CLOAK THE LAND.

THE VILLAGE STILL FLOWS UNDER THE SWAY OF A *BEWITCHING* POWER. IT KEEPS THE TOWNSFOLK IN A DREAM-LIKE STATE.

AND THEY ARE SUBJECT TO *DAYDREAMS*, *TRANCES* AND *VISIONS*.

IT IS A REGULAR OCCURRENCE FOR MOST TO HEAR *VOICES* IN THE SPELLBOUND AIR.

THE ENTIRE VILLAGE BELIEVES IN *GHOST STORIES* AND LOCAL TALES OF *HAUNTED AREAS.*

WHEN THE INKY BLACKNESS OF NIGHT COVERS SLEEPY HOLLOW, IT IS BELIEVED THAT MANY *TORMENTED SPECTRES* AND *MOURNFUL GHOSTS* ARISE. THEY LEAVE THEIR HAUNTED SPACES TO ADD THEIR SUPERNATURAL CHILL TO THE SUNLESS AIR.

BUT OF ALL OF THESE SPIRITS, THERE IS ONE SPECTRE WHO SEEMS TO *CONTROL* ALL THEIR POWERS.

THE DOMINANT SPIRIT IS A FIGURE ON HORSEBACK, CLAD IN BLACK, AND *WITHOUT A HEAD!*

HE HAS OFTEN BEEN SEEN BY MANY OF THE LOCALS, IN AND AROUND THE VILLAGE AND ITS NEIGHBOURING ROADS. AND THIS GHOST WHO RIDES LIKE A MIDNIGHT BLAST IS KNOWN BY ALL AS *THE HEADLESS HORSEMAN OF SLEEPY HOLLOW.*

THUD! THUD! THUD!

Graphic Chillers

THE LEGEND OF SLEEPY HOLLOW

ADAPTED AND ILLUSTRATED BY

JEFF ZORNOW

BASED UPON THE WORKS BY

WASHINGTON IRVING

EDGE FRANKLIN WATTS

LONDON•SYDNEY

THE LEGEND OF SLEEPY HOLLOW

ABOUT THE AUTHOR

Washington Irving was born on 3 April, 1783, in New York City. He was the youngest of 11 children. In 1801, Irving was apprenticed to a lawyer, but he soon got bored.

The following year, Irving had his first story published in the *Morning Chronicle*. He took several trips up the Hudson River, into Canada, and throughout Europe.

In 1806, Irving returned home and passed the bar examination to become a lawyer. However, he spent most of his time writing essays and stories with his brothers. In 1809, he completed the *Knickerbocker History of New York*.

During the next 10 years, Irving was an officer in the War of 1812 and had several jobs in Europe. He never married. In 1819, he published *The Sketch Book of Geoffrey Crayon, Gent*. This collection of stories quickly became a success, especially the short stories in it called *Rip Van Winkle* and *The Legend of Sleepy Hollow*.

Due to the success of the *Sketch Book*, Irving was able to write full time. He returned to the United States in 1832 and continued to write. He died at home in Tarrytown, New York, on 28 November, 1859.

BUT PERHAPS, DEAR READER, THIS STORY WOULD NOT BE TOLD AT ALL IF IT WERE NOT FOR THE ARRIVAL OF THE NEW SCHOOLMASTER, *ICHABOD CRANE*.

A TALL AND LANKY, ALMOST GOOFY LOOKING FELLOW.

WITH NARROW SHOULDERS, AND ARMS THAT HUNG A MILE PAST HIS SLEEVES...

...AND FEET THAT LOOKED LIKE SHOVELS.

HIS HEAD WAS SMALL AND FLAT. HE HAD EARS LIKE AN ELEPHANT'S, LARGE GREEN EYES AND A LONG NOSE. HE LOOKED LIKE A WEATHERVANE POINTING THE DIRECTION OF THE WIND.

THE SCHOOLHOUSE WAS A SIMPLE, ONE-ROOM LOG BUILDING NEXT TO A CREEK. ICHABOD BROUGHT HIS OWN SENSE OF HOW HE WOULD 'ENLIGHTEN' THE YOUTH OF WHAT HE CONSIDERED THESE 'SIMPLE-MINDED' COUNTRY FOLK.

AND ICHABOD WAS NOT THE NICEST TEACHER. GOODNESS NO! HE WAS QUITE *STRICT*, WITH A *FIERCE ATTITUDE* THE CHILDREN HAD NEVER EXPERIENCED BEFORE.

HE WOULD TAKE FULL ADVANTAGE OF THIS. ACTING AS A *KING* RULING OVER HIS SUBJECTS IN THAT CLASSROOM.

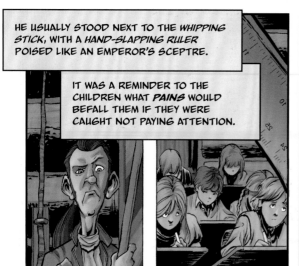

HE USUALLY STOOD NEXT TO THE *WHIPPING STICK*, WITH A *HAND-SLAPPING RULER* POISED LIKE AN EMPEROR'S SCEPTRE.

IT WAS A REMINDER TO THE CHILDREN WHAT *PAINS* WOULD BEFALL THEM IF THEY WERE CAUGHT NOT PAYING ATTENTION.

OUTSIDE THE CLASSROOM, ICHABOD CRANE WOULD WEAR A VERY DIFFERENT FACE. HE DID NOT EARN MUCH MONEY. IT WAS CUSTOM FOR THE TEACHER TO STAY WITH HIS STUDENTS' FAMILIES IN ROTATION FOR A WEEK AT A TIME.

THIS DID NOT PLEASE THE STUDENTS AT ALL!

NOR DID IT PLEASE SOME OF THE SLIGHTLY POORER FAMILIES. FOR ALTHOUGH ICHABOD WAS A VERY SKINNY FELLOW, HE HAD THE *APPETITE OF A PIG!*

AND EATING WAS ONE OF ICHABOD'S *FAVOURITE* PASTIMES.

BUT THERE WERE MORE CURIOUS THINGS TO THIS MAN WHO CLAIMED TO BE OF A 'HIGHER INTELLIGENCE'.

FOR JUST LIKE THOSE NATIVES OF THE HOLLOW, ICHABOD WAS A VERY *SUPERSTITIOUS* FELLOW.

ICHABOD HAD READ SEVERAL BOOKS THOROUGHLY. BUT THE ONE THAT CAPTURED HIS INTEREST THE MOST WAS HIS COPY OF *THE HISTORY OF NEW ENGLAND WITCHCRAFT*. AND *WITCHCRAFT* WAS ONE OF THE MANY THINGS ICHABOD FIRMLY BELIEVED IN.

LA-LA!

LA-LA!

LA-LA!

AWOOO!

AMONG HIS OTHER PASTIMES, ICHABOD FANCIED HIMSELF AS A SINGER. HE TOOK IT UPON HIMSELF TO GIVE THE LADIES CHOIR LESSONS IN SINGING THE CHURCH HYMNS.

EVEN THOUGH IT WAS JOKED BEHIND HIS BACK THAT ICHABOD'S OWN SINGING RESEMBLED THE *HOWLING* OF A *DOG!*

BUT AS ICHABOD WAS CONSIDERED AN EDUCATED GENTLEMAN, HE WAS NOT WHAT THE WOMEN OF SLEEPY HOLLOW WERE *USED* TO. SOON, HE BECAME A RATHER WELCOME FIGURE IN FEMALE SOCIAL CIRCLES.

AND MANY OF ICHABOD'S NIGHTS WERE SPENT WITH THE LADIES TELLING ALL MANNER OF *GHOST STORIES.* THE OLD WIVES DELIGHTED IN TALKING ABOUT THE LOCAL HAUNTS. AND ICHABOD, IN TURN, WOULD *TEASE* AND *FRIGHTEN* THEM WITH STORIES OF WITCHCRAFT FROM HIS BOOK.

HEE-HEE HEE!

HA-HA!

HA-HA!

OOOH!

AT THE END OF ONE SUCH STORYTELLING NIGHT, ICHABOD BEGAN HIS WALK HOME. DURING THAT WALK, ICHABOD'S STRONGEST CHARACTER TRAIT SHOWED THROUGH – HIS NERVOUS *FEAR.*

HIS FEAR OF WHAT UNKNOWN *NIGHTMARES* MAY LIE IN WAIT IN THE DARKNESS OF THE WITCHING HOUR.

IT SEEMED ALL MANNER OF FEARFUL SHADOWS *TORMENTED* ICHABOD ON HIS WALK THROUGH THE BLACKENED WOODS. FOR IT WAS SAID BY EVERYONE IN THE VILLAGE THAT THE WOODS WERE *HAUNTED.* HAUNTED BY MANY DIFFERENT TYPES OF SPECTRE AND IN MANY DIFFERENT PLACES!

SCREEE!

SCREEE!

SCREEE!

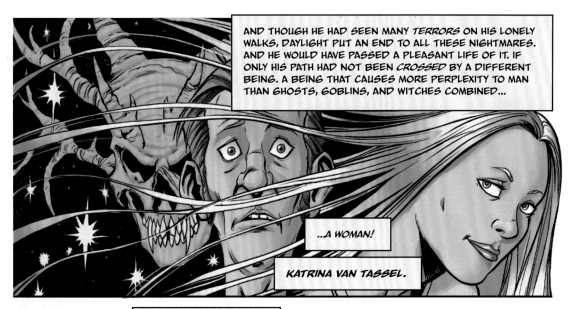

AND THOUGH HE HAD SEEN MANY *TERRORS* ON HIS LONELY WALKS, DAYLIGHT PUT AN END TO ALL THESE NIGHTMARES. AND HE WOULD HAVE PASSED A PLEASANT LIFE OF IT. IF ONLY HIS PATH HAD NOT BEEN *CROSSED* BY A DIFFERENT BEING. A BEING THAT CAUSES MORE PERPLEXITY TO MAN THAN GHOSTS, GOBLINS, AND WITCHES COMBINED...

...A WOMAN!

KATRINA VAN TASSEL.

KATRINA WAS THE ONLY CHILD OF A WEALTHY FARMER, BALTUS VAN TASSEL. ICHABOD NOTICED HER BEAUTY IN HIS SINGING CLASSES.

OH- OH- OH!

AWHOOO!

AND HE CONVINCED HER FAMILY TO GIVE HER *PRIVATE* LESSONS.

KATRINA WAS A FREE-SPIRITED GIRL, CONTENT TO RUN WITH HER FEELINGS.

SHE WAS IN LOVE WITH ALL THE MEN WHO WERE *ENCHANTED* BY HER BEAUTY AND CONFIDENT CHARM.

ICHABOD HAD A SOFT AND FOOLISH HEART TOWARD KATRINA. AND KATRINA, LIKE MANY WOMEN IN THE VILLAGE, FOUND ICHABOD TO BE VERY DIFFERENT FROM THE OTHER MEN. SO, SHE BEGAN TO SPEND TIME GETTING TO KNOW THE SCHOOLTEACHER.

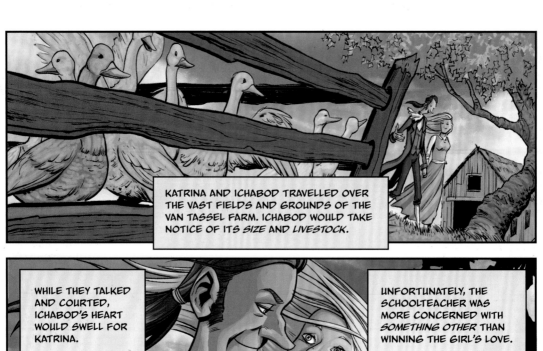

KATRINA AND ICHABOD TRAVELLED OVER THE VAST FIELDS AND GROUNDS OF THE VAN TASSEL FARM. ICHABOD WOULD TAKE NOTICE OF ITS *SIZE* AND *LIVESTOCK*.

WHILE THEY TALKED AND COURTED, ICHABOD'S HEART WOULD SWELL FOR KATRINA.

UNFORTUNATELY, THE SCHOOLTEACHER WAS MORE CONCERNED WITH *SOMETHING OTHER* THAN WINNING THE GIRL'S LOVE.

MMMM!

AND THAT WAS THE WEALTH THAT HE WOULD GAIN IF HE WERE TO *MARRY KATRINA!* THEN EVERY GOOSE COULD BE *COOKED* IN ITS OWN GRAVY. EVERY PIG *ROASTED* WITH A RIPE, RED APPLE IN ITS MOUTH.

EVERY CHICKEN AND TURKEY *BAKED* TO PERFECTION FOR WINTER FEASTS FIT FOR A KINGLY APPETITE SUCH AS ICHABOD'S!

ICHABOD WAS READY TO WIN KATRINA'S HAND IN MARRIAGE. ONLY HE CERTAINLY WAS NOT THE ONLY MAN IN SLEEPY HOLLOW TO PURSUE THE GIRL, FOR SHE DID HAVE OTHER SUITORS.

SUCH AS THE BURLY *BROM BONES.*

SLOSH!

GRRR!

WHUMP!

BROM BONES WAS A *HERO* IN THE COMMUNITY. A ROUGH AND TUMBLE WOODSMAN, HE WAS ALWAYS READY FOR *FUN* OR A *FIGHT!* BUT HE HAD MORE MISCHIEF THAN BAD WILL IN HIS NATURE.

YEH!

BROM!

ALL THE VILLAGERS SPOKE OF BROM'S *ADVENTUROUS* DEEDS AND *WILD* LATE NIGHTS WITH HIS PACK OF FRIENDS.

WHOOP!

WOO-HOO!

CLIP! CLOP!

CLIP!

CLOP!

MEEEEUW!

IT WAS NOT UNCOMMON TO HEAR BROM AND HIS PALS RIDING THROUGH THE VILLAGE *WHOOPING* AND *HOLLERING.* AND ALL THE LADIES WOULD CALL TO HIM CHEERFULLY OUT THEIR WINDOWS.

BROM HAD ALL OF THE LADIES OF SLEEPY HOLLOW AND THE SURROUNDING NEIGHBOURHOODS AT HIS *DISPOSAL*. BUT, IT WAS ONLY KATRINA THAT HE *WANTED*.

HE HAD SPENT YEARS *TRYING* TO WIN HER LOVE. AND KATRINA HAD SPENT YEARS *AVOIDING* HIS ADVANCES. BUT ONLY ENOUGH SO THAT HE WOULD NOT GIVE UP TRYING.

AND NOW THAT BROM SAW KATRINA SPEAKING SO FREELY AND HAPPILY WITH ICHABOD, IT MADE HIM *TERRIBLY JEALOUS!*

HRMPH!

SO BROM ATTEMPTED TO *SCARE* ICHABOD AWAY. HE BEGAN A SERIES OF SPOOKY PRANKS ON THE TEACHER.

WAAAAHH!

ONCE GOING SO FAR AS TO MAKE THE FRIGHTENED ICHABOD THINK THAT WITCHES HAD *CURSED* THE SCHOOLHOUSE!

ONE DAY A SERVANT DELIVERED A PERSONAL LETTER TO ICHABOD AT THE SCHOOL.

ICHABOD'S EYES WIDENED. IT WAS AN INVITATION TO THE VAN TASSEL'S ANNUAL AUTUMN PARTY!

PERSONALLY SENT BY KATRINA!

HUH?

THE CHILDEN LOOKED AT THEIR TEACHER IN STUNNED SILENCE. THEY HAD NEVER SEEN MR CRANE ACT SO... STRANGELY BEFORE.

IN HIS OVERWHELMING JOY, ICHABOD DISMISSED THE CHILDREN EARLY. HE WANTED PLENTY OF TIME TO GET READY FOR THE BIG EVENT.

WOO-HOO!

YAY!

13

ICHABOD PUT ON HIS ONE GOOD SUIT AND COMBED HIS HAIR. HE CHECKED HIS APPPEARANCE IN A SHARD OF BROKEN MIRROR HUNG AT THE BACK OF THE SCHOOLHOUSE.

TO APPEAR EVEN MORE IMPRESSIVE, HE BORROWED A HORSE FROM HANS VAN RIPPER.

GROOMED, DRESSED IN HIS GOOD CLOTHES, AND RIDING ON HIS HORSE, ICHABOD FELT LIKE A *KNIGHT*. HE WAS ON A *QUEST* TO WIN HIS PRINCESS KATRINA!

BUT MY DEAR READER, I MUST POINT OUT JUST HOW *SILLY* OUR HERO APPEARED.

HIS STIRRUPS WERE *TOO* HIGH, WHICH BROUGHT HIS KNEES UP NEARLY TO THE POMMEL OF THE SADDLE. AND HE HELD HIS RIDING CROP LIKE A SCEPTRE – SO HIS ELBOWS WERE OUT TO HIS SIDES AND HIS ARMS RESEMBLED FLAPPING *CHICKEN WINGS*.

AND THE HORSE ICHABOD RODE ON, NAMED *GUNPOWDER*, WAS LITTLE MORE THAN AN OLD BROKEN DOWN PLOUGH HORSE.

GUNPOWDER'S MANE WAS TANGLED, AND ONE OF HIS EYES WAS *BLINDED* WHILE THE OTHER HAD THE GLEAM OF A *DEMON* IN IT. HIS MOUTH HUNG OPEN AND HE WAS PANTING.

AND GUNPOWDER HOBBLED ALONG SLOWLY ON CLUMSY BENT LEGS.

CLUMP! CLUMP!

SNORT!

GAAAWW!
CAAAWW!

IT WAS A BEAUTIFUL AUTUMN AFTERNOON AS ICHABOD RODE TO THE VAN TASSEL PARTY. AND THE FIELDS AND FORESTS WERE RICH WITH FOOD TO BE GATHERED BEFORE WINTER SET IN.

THE COLOURS OF THE TREES WERE FANTASTIC. AND THE SUN SHONE BRIGHTLY, BRINGING WITH IT AN AIR OF WARM PEACEFULNESS.

ICHABOD COULD NOT HELP BUT SMILE DURING HIS SLOW RIDE TO MEET HIS KATRINA.

FOR HE COULD FEEL THE CONFIDENCE THAT THIS NIGHT HE WOULD WIN HER HEART FOREVER.

AND THAT THIS NIGHT WOULD BE A VERY SPECIAL NIGHT.

NKKK!

CLUMP!
CLUMP!

NNNK!

A NIGHT ICHABOD WOULD REMEMBER FOR THE REST OF HIS DAYS.

UPON ARRIVING AT THE VAN TASSEL MANSION, ICHABOD WAS GREETED WARMLY BY KATRINA'S FATHER. HE WAS ENCOURAGED TO JOIN THE REST OF THE PARTY GUESTS IN THE LARGE HALL.

BROM WAS AT THE PARTY...

...AND WAS *NOT* PLEASED TO SEE HIS RIVAL.

ICHABOD DOVE INTO THE IMMENSE AMOUNTS OF CAKES, DOUGHNUTS, PIES AND PASTRIES AVAILABLE.

AND THE MORE FOOD HE ATE, THE HAPPIER HE BECAME.

WHEN THE LOVELY KATRINA ENTERED THE ROOM, BOTH ICHABOD AND BROM FELT A *HEATED SHOCK* INSIDE THEMSELVES.

AND SHE WENT STRAIGHT TO ICHABOD FOR A DANCE. WHICH MADE BROM *FURIOUS* AS A LION!

ESPECIALLY SINCE BIG BROM DID NOT KNOW HOW TO DANCE!

OH! MY DEAR READER, WHAT A *STUNNING SIGHT* KATRINA WAS IN HER NEW PARTY DRESS SHE HAD MADE HERSELF. AND WITH DECORATIVE ORNAMENTS IN HER HAIR SHE FASHIONED OUT OF LEAVES, BERRIES AND WHEAT FROM THE HARVEST. KATRINA APPEARED AS AN *AUTUMN FAIRY*, WHO HAD FLOWN DOWN FROM THE WOODS TO GRACE THE EVENT WITH HER MERRY SPIRIT.

SHE AND ICHABOD ENJOYED THEIR DANCE. AS DID ALL THE GUESTS WHO COULD NOT LOOK AWAY FROM THE SPLENDID SIGHT OF KATRINA.

BROM BONES WAS SORELY SMITTEN WITH *LOVE* AND *JEALOUSY*. HE STOOD IN A CORNER BROODING.

WEEE! HEEE! HAAR!

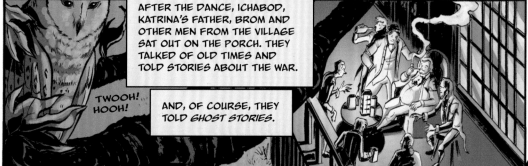

AFTER THE DANCE, ICHABOD, KATRINA'S FATHER, BROM AND OTHER MEN FROM THE VILLAGE SAT OUT ON THE PORCH. THEY TALKED OF OLD TIMES AND TOLD STORIES ABOUT THE WAR.

TWOOH! HOOH!

AND, OF COURSE, THEY TOLD *GHOST STORIES*.

SOON THE MEN WERE DISCUSSING THE MOST FAMOUS LOCAL GHOST...

...THE *HEADLESS HORSEMAN!*

OLD MAN BROUWER INSISTED THAT HE HAD *SEEN* HIM ONCE WITH HIS OWN EYES.

WAHHHHHH!

OLD BROUWER TOLD HIS STORY OF HOW THE HORSEMAN CAME UP TO CHASE HIM NEAR THE OLD DUTCH CHURCH CEMETERY.

CLICK! CLACK!

AND ONCE OLD BROUWER HAD CROSSED THE BRIDGE NEARBY, THE HORSEMAN STOPPED. UNABLE TO CROSS, HE TURNED INTO A *SKELETON* AND *DISAPPEARED.*

THEN BROM BONES TOLD A STORY OF HIS OWN. ONE EVEN MORE *FANTASTIC* THAN OLD BROUWER'S.

GULP!

THE STORIES WERE HAVING THEIR *TERRIFYING* EFFECT ON ICHABOD.

BROM'S STORY HAPPENED ONE NIGHT NEAR THE SAME OLD CHURCH. THE *HEADLESS HORSEMAN* RODE DOWN OUT OF THE BLACK SKY AND BRAVE BROM CHALLENGED HIM TO A RACE.

THE WINNER WOULD RECEIVE THREE BOTTLES OF THE FINEST CIDER IN THE HOLLOW.

THE TWO RACED OVER BUSH AND DITCH, OVER HILL AND SWAMP. AND BROM TEASED THE HORSEMAN ALL THE WAY.

BROM SIGHED ONCE HE GOT TO THE PART IN HIS TALE WHEN THEY REACHED THE BRIDGE.

FZZZZT!

SNORT!

SNORT!

THERE, THE HEADLESS HORSEMAN RODE A *BOLT OF LIGHTNING* BACK UP INTO THE SKY.

BROM FELT HE WAS CHEATED IN THE RACE.

SOON THE PARTY BROKE UP, AND THE LAST OF THE GUESTS WERE LEAVING.

ICHABOD STAYED BEHIND SO THAT HE COULD HAVE A SERIOUS HEART-TO-HEART WITH KATRINA.

HE WAS CONVINCED THAT HE WAS ON THE HIGH ROAD TO *SUCCESS*. THIS WAS THE MOMENT HE WOULD POUR OUT HIS *FEELINGS* FOR KATRINA AND SHE WOULD *EXPRESS* HER LOVE FOR HIM.

DEAR READER, WHAT WAS SAID IN THIS CONVERSATION I DO NOT KNOW.

BUT I FEAR THAT SOMETHING MUST HAVE GONE WRONG! FOR POOR ICHABOD LEFT AFTER ONLY A FEW MOMENTS, AND WAS LOOKING QUITE UPSET.

=HUF=

SNIFF!
SNIFF!

WITH COLD, SILENT TEARS RUNNING DOWN HIS FACE, ICHABOD MADE HIS HEAVY-HEARTED WAY HOMEWARD.

THROUGH THE INKY BLACKNESS OF NIGHT.

AT THE HEIGHT OF THE WITCHING HOUR.

FAR BELOW ICHABOD RAN THE TAPPAN ZEE RIVER. ITS COOL WATERS REFLECTED THE MOONLIT SCENE ALL AROUND HIM. A SCENE AS DARK AND GLOOMY AS ICHABOD HIMSELF FELT.

CLUMP! CLUMP!

SHHHHHM SHHHHHM

CAAW!

≷RIP≷

CROAK!

ICHABOD HAD NEVER FELT QUITE SO ALONE, AND NOW THE NIGHT SEEMED TO GET DARKER AND DARKER.

CAAW! CAAW!

ICHABOD WAS APPROACHING A *HAUNTED SPOT* FROM MANY OF THE LOCAL GHOST STORIES HE HAD HEARD.

MAJOR ANDRE'S TREE.

A *MONSTOUS* AND *GNARLED* TREE WHERE MANY BATS AND RAVENS MADE THEIR HOME.

THE *OLD NOOSE* USED TO HANG ANDRE STILL SWAYED IN THE COLD WIND.

TWANG!

SOMETHING SCARED GUNPOWDER AND HE REARED UP AND SPAT!

NEEEH!

ICHABOD TRIED HIS BEST TO CALM THE OLD HORSE.

BUT THE SCHOOLTEACHER WAS QUITE SCARED HIMSELF.

THIS NIGHT SEEMED TO BE FILLED WITH DEVILRY!

ABOUT 50 METRES AWAY FROM ANDRE'S TREE, ICHABOD WAS STILL TRYING TO CALM DOWN GUNPOWDER. THE OLD HORSE SEEMED TO MOVE AT A VERY *ODD* AND *UNCERTAIN* PACE.

IT WAS AS IF HE WAS NOW AFRAID OF ANOTHER *UNSEEN NIGHTMARE*.

TO EASE THE TENSION, ICHABOD WHISTLED A HYMNM. SUDDENLY ANOTHER COLD BREEZE PICKED UP. THEN GUNPOWDER SLOWED ALMOST TO A HALT.

PEEP
PIP

WHOOOSH!

AND THEN, TRAVELLING RIGHT BESIDE ICHABOD WAS...*SOMETHING*...

SOMETHING *HUGE*...

AND *MISSHAPEN*...

AND *BLACK* AND *TOWERING*.

ICHABOD WAS SCARED STIFF AND DID NOT KNOW WHAT TO DO! SO HE GATHERED UP THE COURAGE TO SPEAK TO THE NEW TRAVELLER.

SNORT!
SNORT!

THUD!
THUD!

AND INTO THE HAUNTED NIGHT THE TWO RIDERS RACED. THOUGH ICHABOD WAS A VERY UNSKILLED RIDER, THIS SEEMED TO GIVE HIM AN ADVANTAGE IN THE CHASE.

WHOOOSH!

THUD!
THUD!
THUD!
CLOMP! CLOMP!

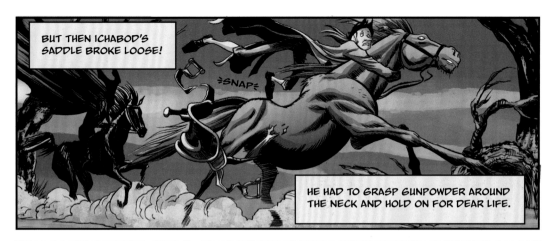

BUT THEN ICHABOD'S SADDLE BROKE LOOSE!

=SNAP=

HE HAD TO GRASP GUNPOWDER AROUND THE NECK AND HOLD ON FOR DEAR LIFE.

BUT OLD GUNPOWDER PROVED THAT HE *WAS* POSSESSED BY A DEMON.

THEY PASSED THE OLD DUTCH CHURCH, BUT GUNPOWDER TURNED LEFT OFF THE ROAD TOWARD SLEEPY HOLLOW.

THIS DOWNHILL ROAD LED THROUGH A SANDY WOODED HOLLOW. UNDER A CANOPY OF TREES, IT CROSSED THE BRIDGE IN THE HEADLESS HORSEMAN TALES. ICHABOD KNEW IF HE COULD REACH THE BRIDGE, HE WOULD BE SAFE.

BUT HE COULD FEEL THE *BREATH* OF THE BLACK HORSE JUST BEHIND HIM!

27

GUNPOWDER THUNDERED ACROSS THE BRIDGE.

ICHABOD TURNED TO LOOK BEHIND HIM. HE WANTED TO SEE IF THE HEADLESS HORSEMAN WOULD INDEED *VANISH* IN A FLASH OF FIRE OR LIGHTNING.

ONLY THAT DID NOT HAPPEN!

HUH?

THE HORSEMAN THREW HIS DECAYED HEAD ACROSS THE BRIDGE!

IT STRUCK POOR ICHABOD CRANE'S SKULL LIKE A CANNONBALL!

SHLUMP!

THE NEXT MORNING, GUNPOWDER WAS FOUND OUTSIDE HANS VAN RIPPER'S HOME WITHOUT HIS SADDLE. ICHABOD WAS NOWHERE TO BE FOUND.

A SEARCH FOUND ICHABOD'S TRAIL AND IT WAS FOLLOWED FROM THE OLD BRIDGE. ON THE BANK BESIDE THE CREEK, THE HAT OF THE UNFORTUNATE ICHABOD WAS FOUND. IT WAS COVERED IN THE REMAINS OF A SMASHED AND ROTTED PUMPKIN.

ICHABOD CRANE HIMSELF WAS *NEVER* SEEN AGAIN.

NEEEEIGH!

THE MYSTERIOUS *DISAPPEARANCE* OF ICHABOD LED TO MUCH *GOSSIP* AND MANY *RUMOURS*. AND ALL THE STORIES OF THE HEADLESS HORSEMAN WERE RECALLED.

BROM BONES MARRIED KATRINA SOON AFTER. AND WHENEVER THE SUBJECT OF THE STRANGE VANISHING OF THE SCHOOLTEACHER WAS BROUGHT UP, BROM WOULD LAUGH HEARTILY. THIS MADE SOME FOLKS GOSSIP *MORE*.

BUT THE OLD COUNTRY WIVES ARE THE BEST JUDGES IN THESE MATTERS. THEY INSISTED THAT ICHABOD CRANE WAS CARRIED AWAY BY *SUPERNATURAL* POWERS! AND THE STORY WAS PASSED ON.

AND IT IS TO THIS VERY DAY A FAVOURITE STORY TOLD OFTEN AROUND THE NEIGHBOURHOOD FIRESIDES. IT WILL CONTINUE FOREVERMORE TO BE THE LEGEND OF SLEEPY HOLLOW.

THE END.

This edition first published in 2010 by
Franklin Watts
338 Euston Road
London NW1 3BH

Franklin Watts Australia
Level 17/207 Kent Street
Sydney NSW 2000

Copyright © 2008 Abdo Consulting Group, Inc.

First published in the USA by Magic Wagon, a division of the ABDO Group

1 3 5 7 9 10 8 6 4 2

Based upon the works of Washington Irving
Written and illustrated by Jeff Zornow
Letters and colours by Lynx Studios
Edited and directed by Chazz DeMoss
Cover design by Neil Klinepier
UK cover design by Peter Scoulding

A CIP catalogue record for this book is available from the British Library.

Dewey number: 741.5

ISBN: 978 0 7496 9687 0

Printed in China

Franklin Watts is a division of Hachette Children's Books,
an Hachette UK company.
www.hachette.co.uk

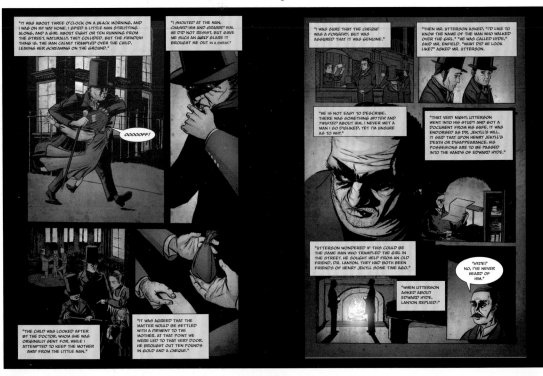

READ THE REST OF THIS STORY IN: DR. JEKYLL AND MR. HYDE